The SHIVERS in the FRIDGE

by FRAN MANUSHKIN

Illustrated by PAUL O. ZELINSKY

Dutton Children's Books
New York

"**Brrr!** It's cold today!" groaned Papa Shivers.

"*I'll* say!" chimed in Mama Shivers.

"SHIVER MY BONES! IT'S COLD!" roared Grandpa.

Sonny, the youngest, said, "It's been c-c-cold ever since we got here—and dark."

"This *is* a strange place to live," moaned Grandma, "with the monsters and all."

"Watch out!" warned Grandpa, sniffing the air. "My old bones feel an earthquake coming! Everybody—*hide*!"

Sure enough, the whole world began to shake, and a great blazing
light shone forth. The Shivers shook with fear as a monster appeared!
Its long, long claws r e a c h e d   o u t,

r e a c h e d   o u t—

then *PHOOMPH!!!* The earthquake was over, the monster was gone, and the Shivers were plunged back into darkness.

"Is everyone all right?" Papa called. He lined up the family and counted: "One-two-three-four-*FIVE* cold noses. Everyone's f-f-fine."

"I wonder what the monster snatched this time?" said Sonny. "Look! Cheesy Square is gone."

"How you can see in the dark is beyond me," groaned Grandma.

"SHIVER MY BONES!" Grandpa roared. "I feel another earthquake coming! Everybody—*hide!*"

Sure enough, the whole world began to shake, and a great blazing light shone forth. Another monster reached out, r e a c h e d o u t—then *PHOOMPH!!!*

The earthquake was over, the monster was gone, and the Shivers were plunged back into darkness.

Sonny shouted, "Look! Cheesy Square is back, and so is J-J-JELLY."

"Sonny, don't read in the dark," warned Mama. "You'll ruin your eyes."

Papa sighed. "Sometimes I think this is a strange place to live."

"Now, now," Mama assured him. "No place is perfect."

At bedtime, the family huddled together for warmth in their cardboard box.

Sonny begged, "Mama, tell me a story."

"I'll t-t-try," said Mama, and through chattering teeth, she began: "Once upon a time there was a warm and cozy family. The m-m-mama was warm, the p-p-papa was cozy, the—*OUCH!*"

Grandma was poking Mama with her pointy elbow. "Don't fill the boy's head with nonsense," she scolded. "Cold we are and cold we'll *always* be."

But the next morning, Papa pondered, "Maybe Mama's right, and there *is* a warmer place to live. I'll search the world until I find it."

Boldly, Papa marched into the darkness. He squeezed past Orange Hills, tiptoed around Egg Valley, and—oops! He tripped on Buttery Cliff. And that's when an earthquake struck.

The whole world wobbled and the great light glared.

A monster reached out, r e a c h e d   o u t—then *PHOOMPH!!!* When it was over, Egg Valley, Buttery Cliff—and PAPA!—were gone. Sonny asked hopefully, "Will Papa come back like J-J-JELLY always does?"

"I don't know," Mama moaned, wringing her frosty hands. "The monsters never found us before."

All that day there were earthquakes galore, but none of them brought back Papa. The Shivers family wept cold, cold tears.

KEEP REFRIGERATED
A • PASTEURIZED • HOMOGENIZED
trition Facts
Size One Cup 236mL
per Container 4
r Serving

At bedtime, they huddled together in their
cardboard box, leaving an empty place for Papa.
Sonny begged, "Mama, tell me a story."
Through chattering teeth, Mama sighed, "I'll
t-t-try: Once upon a time there was a family who
stood tall and proud. The m-m-mama stood tall,
the p-p-papa stood proud, the—*OUCH!*"
Grandma was poking Mama with her pointy knee.
"Don't fill Sonny's head with tall tales," she scolded.
Then everyone had a cold night's sleep.

The next morning Grandpa declared, "Maybe Mama's right, and there *is* a place we can stand tall. I'm going to find it—and Papa too!"

"Stop!" Grandma gave him a sour look. "Don't get into a pickle!"

But Grandpa began his daring journey. With tear-filled eyes, he trekked through Onion Circles. Sneezing and wheezing, he rushed past Horseradish Ridge and climbed to the snowy peak of Mt. Ketchup.

"Ahoy there!" he called jauntily. Then, "Uh-oh!" he yelled. "I'm stuck! I can't move!"

Alas, that's when an earthquake struck!
Mt. Ketchup trembled and teetered and the
furious light blazed, and a monster reached out,
r e a c h e d   o u t—
And when it was over—PHOOMPH!!! Onion
Circles, Mt. Ketchup—and GRANDPA!—were gone.

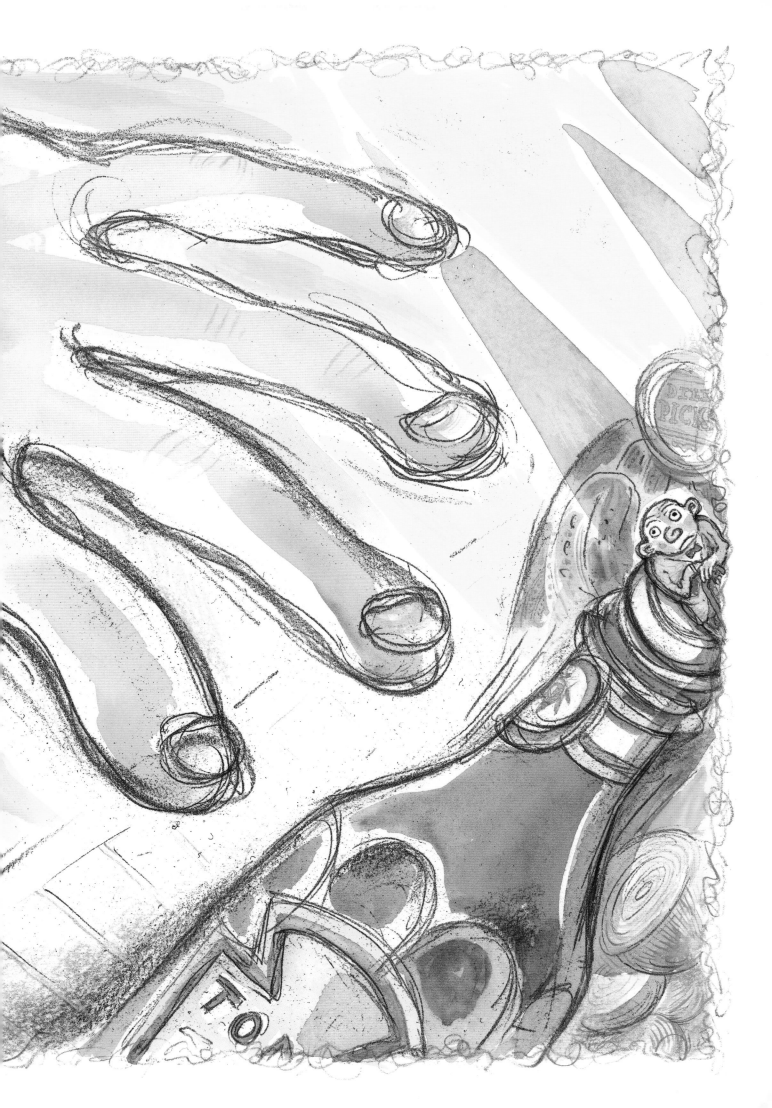

"See what comes of standing tall?" Grandma grumbled.

"Papa *and* Grandpa gone!" cried Sonny.

At bedtime, the Shivers left two empty places in their cardboard box.

"One, two, three cold noses," counted Mama.

"Tell me a story," Sonny begged.

Through chattering teeth, Mama said, "I'll t-t-try: Once upon a t-t-time there was a family who were brave and strong. The p-p-papa was brave, the m-m-mama was strong, the—*OUCH!*"

Grandma was poking Mama with her pointy toes. "Baloney!" she grunted. "Stop talking such applesauce!"

The next day brought—OH, NO!—another earthquake. *PHOOMPH!!!* When it was over, Mama found something new: a clear Emerald Lake.

"Oh, my," she murmured. "It looks w-w-warm." Saucily, Mama dipped a toe in. "It *is* warm," she marveled. And with one wild leap, Mama plunged right in. "I'm so comfy." She beamed. "I could stay here forever!"

Mama didn't know how right she was, for Emerald Lake began freezing up, and Mama got stuck in—tight! And then—guess what?

An earthquake struck! The whole world shuddered and the great light shone, and a monster reached out, r e a c h e d   o u t— then *PHOOMPH!!!*

Emerald Lake, Jolly Whip—and MAMA!—were gone.

Grandma shook her pointy finger. "That's what comes of looking for warmth!"

Sonny shivered. "Grandma, now it's just you and m-m-me."

At bedtime, they left three empty places in their cardboard box.

"Grandma," begged Sonny, "tell me a story."

"I don't know any," she said. "Shush now, and shiver yourself to sleep."

The next day, Grandma got up dark and early.
"I've found us the perfect hiding place!" she shouted.
"Spooky Jungle!"

"Not Spooky Jungle!" Sonny shivered.

"Yes!" Grandma insisted, and she wedged herself in nice and tight.

And wouldn't you know it? Yes, indeed! An earth-quake struck! The world tottered, the great light beamed, a monster reached out, r e a c h e d   o u t—

And *PHOOMPH!!!* When Sonny looked around, what did he see? Mt. Mayo, Spooky Jungle—and GRANDMA!—were gone. Now Sonny was all alone! No Mama, no Papa, no Grandma, no Grandpa. Sonny hugged his Honey Bear for comfort, but all he got was sticky.

At bedtime, Sonny shivered in the cardboard box. "Only one cold nose," he counted. There was nobody to tell Sonny a story, so he made one up: "Once upon a time there was a b-b-brave and strong and h-h-happy family! They weren't scared of monsters and were always w-w-warm."

That night, Sonny slept so well, he woke up with a cool look in his eye and a mind as sharp as mustard.

"No more cold feet for me!" he decided. "I'm going to face those monsters and make them give my family back!"

Quickly, Sonny scooted up Purple Boulders. "The monsters are *always* snatching these," he said. "And the next time they do, I'll be waiting!"

Standing tall, Sonny waited,

and waited,

and waited.

At last! An earthquake struck. The whole world joggled, and the fierce light blazed, and a monster reached out, r e a c h e d o u t—and snatched—Purple Boulders! Up flew Sonny, up, up into the light!

Standing tall, Sonny Shivers faced that monster—
and the monster SMILED!

"Mom!" shouted the monster. "Look what I found!
The last magnet!"

"Good for you," said its mother. "I wonder how they
got INTO the fridge?"

Suddenly, Sonny was flying again. Then *PLUNK!*
He landed, and what did he see?

His family! Mama and Papa and Grandma and Grandpa—all standing tall!!

Oh, what a warm reunion they had! Even Grandma smiled!

"Sonny, you were so brave!" praised Mama.

Grandpa grinned. "I *knew* we were made of stronger stuff."

"For sure!" added Papa. "We keep this whole world running."

"And there's so much to *read!*" Sonny marveled.

Then, warm, strong, and happy,
the little family stood tall and proud,
and they never *ever* shivered again!

cream cheese
jelly
oranges
eggs
butter
onions
pickles
horseradish
ketchup
baloney
applesauce
gelatin pudding
whipped cream
celery
mayonnaise
honey
mustard
grapes

DUTTON CHILDREN'S BOOKS
A division of Penguin Young Readers Group

Published by the Penguin Group

Penguin Group (USA) Inc., 375 Hudson Street, New York, New York 10014, U.S.A.
Penguin Group (Canada), 90 Eglinton Avenue East, Suite 700, Toronto, Ontario, Canada M4P 2Y3
(a division of Pearson Penguin Canada Inc.) • Penguin Books Ltd, 80 Strand, London WC2R 0RL,
England • Penguin Ireland, 25 St Stephen's Green, Dublin 2, Ireland (a division of Penguin Books Ltd)
Penguin Group (Australia), 250 Camberwell Road, Camberwell, Victoria 3124, Australia (a division of
Pearson Australia Group Pty Ltd) • Penguin Books India Pvt Ltd, 11 Community Centre, Panchsheel
Park, New Delhi - 110 017, India • Penguin Group (NZ), Cnr Airborne and Rosedale Roads, Albany,
Auckland 1310, New Zealand (a division of Pearson New Zealand Ltd) • Penguin Books (South Africa)
(Pty) Ltd, 24 Sturdee Avenue, Rosebank, Johannesburg 2196, South Africa • Penguin Books Ltd,
Registered Offices: 80 Strand, London WC2R 0RL, England

Text copyright © 2006 by Fran Manushkin
Illustrations copyright © 2006 by Paul O. Zelinsky

Library of Congress Cataloging-in-Publication Data

Manushkin, Fran.
The Shivers in the fridge / by Fran Manushkin ; illustrated by Paul O. Zelinsky.—1st ed.   p. cm.
Summary: One-by-one, the members of the Shivers family disappear
from the inside of their chilly refrigerator home.
ISBN 0-525-46943-5 (alk. paper)
[1. Refrigerators—Fiction. 2. Magnets—Fiction.] I. Zelinsky, Paul O., ill. II. Title.
PZ7.M3195Shi 2006   [E]—dc22 2006003867

Published in the United States by Dutton Children's Books,
a division of Penguin Young Readers Group
345 Hudson Street, New York, New York 10014
www.penguin.com/youngreaders
Designed by Paul O. Zelinsky and Sara Reynolds

Manufactured in China • First Edition
3 5 7 9 10 8 6 4 2

For Deborah M. Hautzig
— F.M.

For Donna Brooks —
for umpteen years of insight and
inspiration —
P.Z.